Dr. Drabble's Phenomenal Antigravity Dust Machine

Written by
Sigmund Brouwer and Wayne Davidson
Illustrated by
Bill Bell

VICTOR BOOKS®
A DIVISION OF SCRIPTURE PRESS PUBLICATIONS INC.
USA CANADA ENGLAND

With love, to
Colette, Justine,
and PJ

ISBN: 0-89693-901-4

VICTOR BOOKS
A division of SP Publications, Inc.
Wheaton, Illinois 60187

Just after Dr. Drabble's Brilliant All-in-One Traveling Apparatus landed in England, the children went to PJ's room.

They began to hang up a picture of their pet skunk Wesley's favorite food.

PJ held the nail in place for Chelsea. She swung hard.

"Ouch," PJ shouted. "It hurts my thumb when you miss!"

Chelsea giggled and accidentally missed again.

"Maybe this isn't such a good idea," she suggested. "Why don't we see if Dr. Drabble has a new invention?"

PJ and Chelsea were traveling around the world with their missionary parents and a genius inventor named Dr. Drabble.

Dr. Drabble's best invention was his Brilliant All-in-One Traveling Apparatus, which was part ship, part bus, and part space shuttle.

He had an assistant named Arnie Clodbuckle and a special laboratory that PJ and Chelsea visited often with Wesley.

The children headed for Dr. Drabble's laboratory.

When they opened the door, they only saw Dr. Drabble. He had a hair dryer in his hand.

"Oh, my," he said as he looked up. "I didn't foresee this problem."

PJ and Chelsea looked up too.

"Arnie," Chelsea exclaimed with delight. "I didn't know you could fly!"

"I can't," he moaned. "This makes me feel funny."

PJ asked Dr. Drabble, "What is happening?"

Dr. Drabble waved his hair dryer. "Watch." He pointed it at Wesley, and it blew out a funny dust.

"This," he said, "sprays Phenomenal Antigravity Dust."

Wesley began to float up in the air.

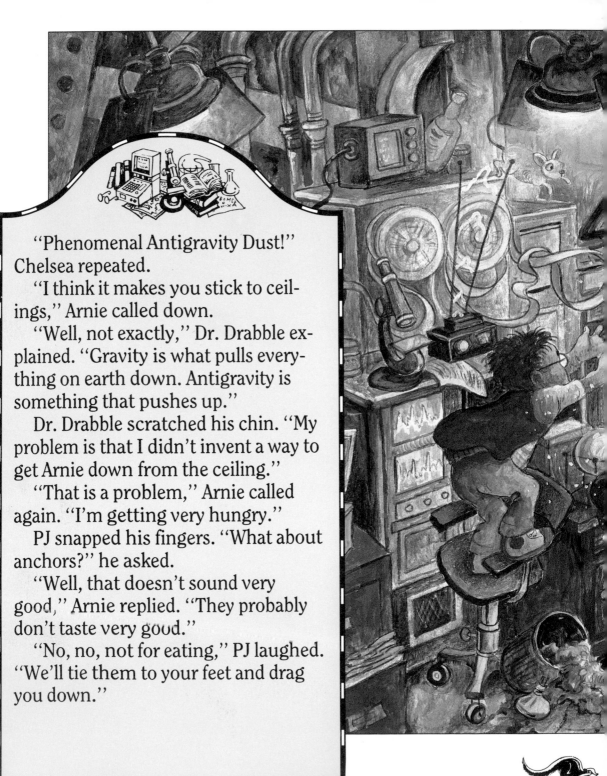

"Phenomenal Antigravity Dust!" Chelsea repeated.

"I think it makes you stick to ceilings," Arnie called down.

"Well, not exactly," Dr. Drabble explained. "Gravity is what pulls everything on earth down. Antigravity is something that pushes up."

Dr. Drabble scratched his chin. "My problem is that I didn't invent a way to get Arnie down from the ceiling."

"That is a problem," Arnie called again. "I'm getting very hungry."

PJ snapped his fingers. "What about anchors?" he asked.

"Well, that doesn't sound very good," Arnie replied. "They probably don't taste very good."

"No, no, not for eating," PJ laughed. "We'll tie them to your feet and drag you down."

Later that day, PJ and Chelsea were alone in the laboratory.

"I have an idea," Chelsea said with a grin. "Let's make a Phenomenal Antigravity Dust Flying Wagon."

Before PJ could say anything, Chelsea was already spraying Phenomenal Antigravity Dust on their wagon.

It started to rise. She jumped in and PJ followed her. She guided the wagon out an open door and soon they were in the sky.

The wagon rose higher and higher until the towns and fields looked very tiny. There were clear streams and tall trees and all kinds of animals. A bird rose in the air with them for a while, very strong and free.

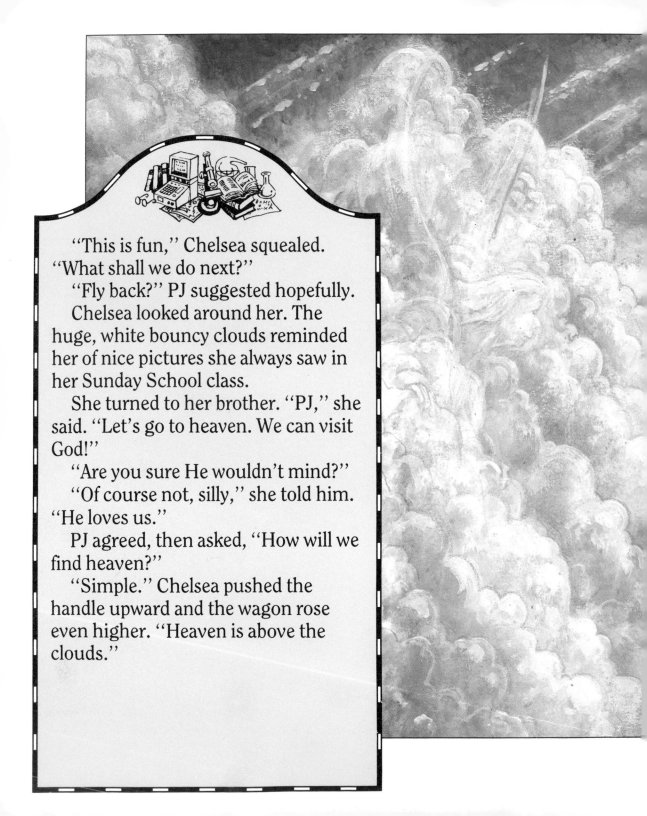

"This is fun," Chelsea squealed. "What shall we do next?"

"Fly back?" PJ suggested hopefully.

Chelsea looked around her. The huge, white bouncy clouds reminded her of nice pictures she always saw in her Sunday School class.

She turned to her brother. "PJ," she said. "Let's go to heaven. We can visit God!"

"Are you sure He wouldn't mind?"

"Of course not, silly," she told him. "He loves us."

PJ agreed, then asked, "How will we find heaven?"

"Simple." Chelsea pushed the handle upward and the wagon rose even higher. "Heaven is above the clouds."

As they rose, the cloud began to grow darker. Then it turned purple. Cold winds started to push them in all directions.

When they reached an opening in the cloud, they saw how terrible the storm was. Purple clouds were everywhere.

A terrifying bright light flashed in their eyes.

KAA-BOOOOOOOOOMM! KAA-BOOOOOOOMMM!

More lightning bolts shot around the tiny wagon, and it began to rain.

Chelsea hugged her brother. "This wind might push us anywhere! I'm sorry I had this idea!"

PJ was praying. "Oh, God, please help us."

Then the wagon was blown sideways and both of them closed their eyes.

After a long while, they hit something solid, and for a moment they were afraid to open their eyes again.

Finally, Chelsea dared to peek a tiny bit with her left eye. Then with her right.

All she saw was a very, very huge building. It was made of ancient stones, and sparkled in the sunlight.

"PJ, PJ, open your eyes. I think we're in heaven!"

Then PJ opened his eyes. All he looked at was the amazing building. Beautiful music floated out from the large, open doorway.

"You're right," he said. "God might be in there."

They were in such a hurry, they did not look around. Otherwise, they might have decided they were really in England again.

When they were inside, they discovered the beautiful music was coming from singers in long white gowns.

"Angels," whispered PJ.

"Yes," Chelsea agreed. "All these other people must really like to be here in heaven."

PJ pulled on the sleeve of a man who was smiling at them.

"Pardon me, sir, but may we see God now?"

The man looked down, then his eyes got very big and he knelt down beside the children. "Are you PJ and Chelsea?"

"Yes," PJ answered. "Is God expecting us?"

"Not exactly," the man laughed. "This is a church, England's famous Westminster Cathedral. But some very worried parents have been asking everybody if they have seen two lost children. They showed me your picture."

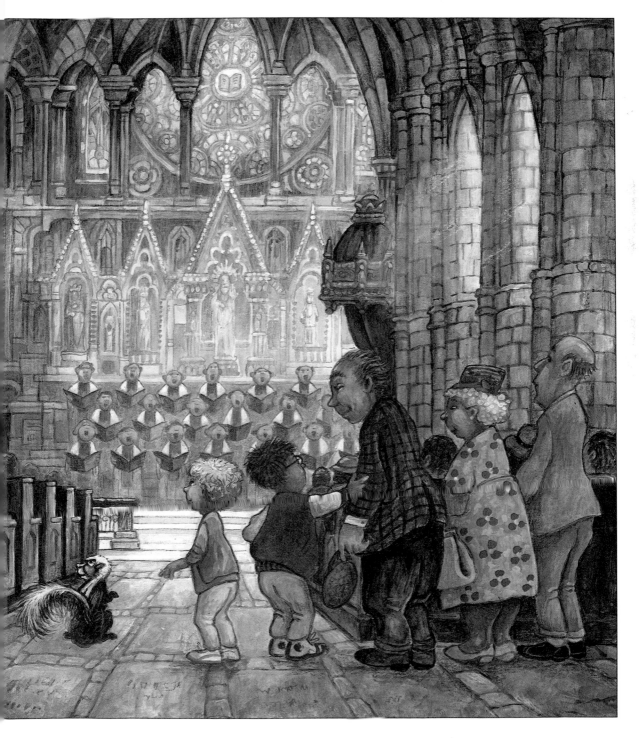

Then the man brought them into a room nearby. Mom and Dad hugged PJ and Chelsea.

"Where have you been?" Dad asked.

The children explained how they had tried to visit God.

Dr. Drabble, who was also very happy to see the children again, said, "I'm afraid it isn't possible that way."

"I'll say," Chelsea frowned. "We didn't find Him anywhere."

PJ added, "We saw cliffs and birds and animals and a scary thunderstorm and a very beautiful church, but we didn't see God once."

"Come here, children," Dad said. He put his arms around both of them. "Let's head back to Dr. Drabble's Brilliant All-in-One Traveling Apparatus. On the way, let me tell you where you might find God."

"The hills and the water and the animals you saw were made perfectly," Dad began to explain. "You saw God working in that perfect beauty."

"The birds were so free," Mom continued. "You saw God's handiwork there too."

"The miles and miles of fields and cities you saw are in God's care," Dad said. "All of it as far as you can see! God is there too."

"Most of all," Mom said with another hug, "God was with you. He let you return to us safely."

PJ and Chelsea understood. God loved them completely and was around them every minute.

Dr. Drabble came up behind them. "You'll have to wait to see God," he said. He grinned and started unfolding some things he'd taken out of his pocket. "But maybe these will be fun while you're waiting . . . I call them my Fantastic Flapping Wingfans."